Pudding Bat's Big Night Out

Written and Illustrated by
Isabella Bunny Bennett

For Tiberius

A Pudding Bat, A Pudding Bat,
A fruit or bug he would have spat
Until he found, one darkened night
Two pudding cups of such delight.

Oh Pudding Bat, Oh Pudding Bat!
Where will you find more sweets like that?
While living in your graveyard home
There's naught but cobwebs, bones, and stone

His parents told him not to fuss,
To eat the moths when it was dusk.
His moms were off to see a play

"Mommy, Mama, please won't you stay?"

His mothers had left for the night,
So Pudding Bat snuck out in flight
To seek another pudding cup!
He asked the Ice Cream Ghost, *"What's up?!"*

"No Pudding Bat, No Pudding Bat,
This is not where your treat is at.
I am the ghost of frozen creams.
Of toppled cones and broken dreams."

"You want this treat? Find one who knows:
A rat lives in the trash dispose.
Surely a creature of such stuff
Could bring to you more than enough!"

High above the starry sky
Streaks the little batty-by
A rumble in his tummy gut
Off to seek the garbage rut

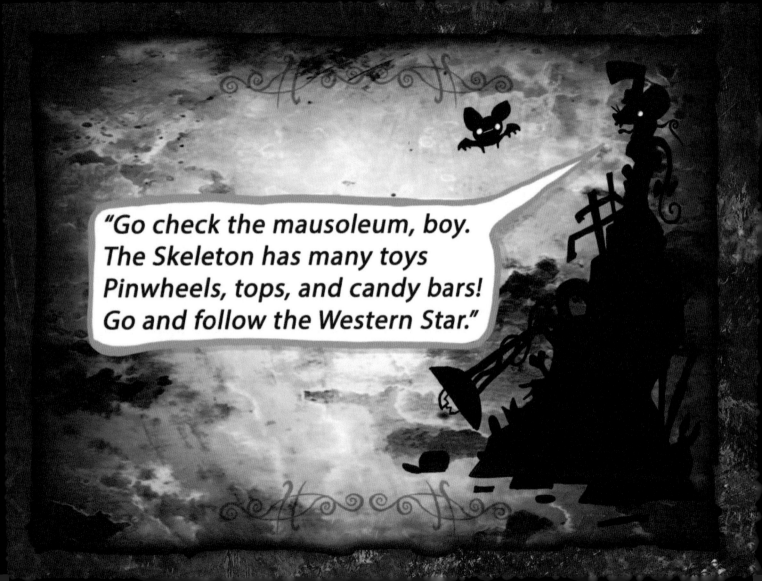

The little bat made such great haste,
A pudding cup he could almost taste!
But this lead was no help at all,
Skeleton laughed and then guffawed:

"Yet if you're wise and if you're keen
In the oak she is sometimes seen
Cleaning all her little paws
And sharpening her sharp, sharp claws."

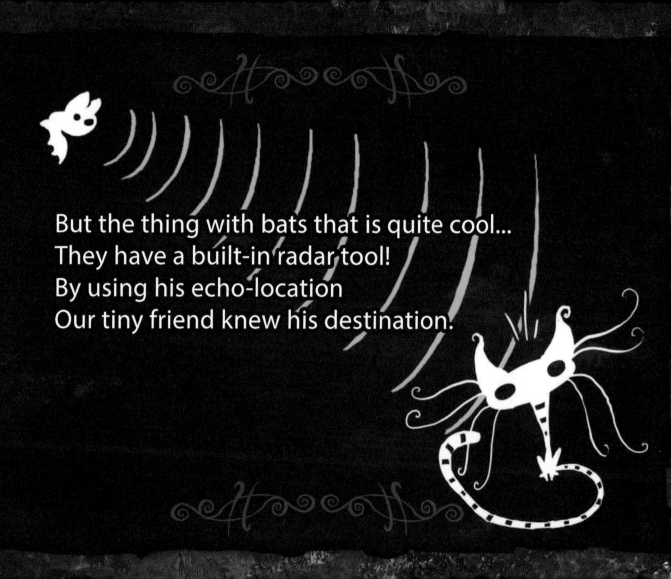

But the thing with bats that is quite cool...
They have a built-in radar tool!
By using his echo-location
Our tiny friend knew his destination.

"Sweet Pudding Bat, Sweet Pudding Bat
Why do you follow me, you brat?
I have no pudding here for you
I did not take it! Go away! Shoo!"

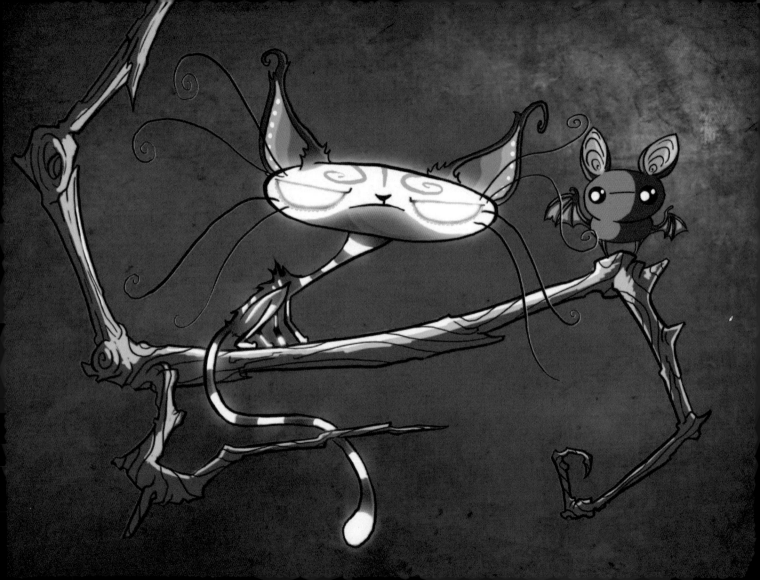

"Skeleton has no eyes to see!
He confused someone else for me.
The zombie bunny, that poor soul,
Hoards his treats in a rabbit hole."

Could Pudding Bat, in chill night's calm,
Get on home before his two moms?
He worried it would be too late...
Maybe pudding was not his fate.

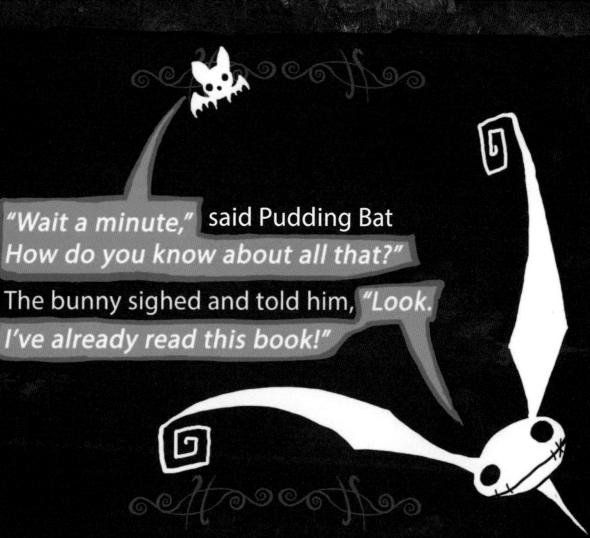

"To the play, your parents did go
But it was cancelled, don't you know?
So go fly quickly to your pad
Maybe your parents won't be mad!"

Poor Pudding Bat, Poor Pudding Bat,
Your cups of sweet have made you fat.
Why did you spend all night in search?
Good little bats stay home and perch.

"Oh Pudding Bat, Oh Pudding Bat,
Don't just go flying off like that!
Your Mommies love you much, my dear.
For your safety we'll always fear."

"It's all the same," replied Mama.
"There was no need for the drama.
Have some patience and clean your plate.
Pudding comes to those who wait!"

THE END

Printed in Great Britain
by Amazon.co.uk, Ltd.,
Marston Gate.